D0339948

Dear Parent:
Your child's love of reading starts here!

Every child learns to read in a different way and at his or her own speed. Some go back and forth between reading levels and read favorite books again and again. Others read through each level in order. You can help your young reader improve and become more confident by encouraging his or her own interests and abilities. From books your child reads with you to the first books he or she reads alone, there are I Can Read Books for every stage of reading:

SHARED READING
Basic language, word repetition, and whimsical illustrations, ideal for sharing with your emergent reader

BEGINNING READING
Short sentences, familiar words, and simple concepts for children eager to read on their own

READING WITH HELP
Engaging stories, longer sentences, and language play for developing readers

READING ALONE
Complex plots, challenging vocabulary, and high-interest topics for the independent reader

ADVANCED READING
Short paragraphs, chapters, and exciting themes for the perfect bridge to chapter books

I Can Read Books have introduced children to the joy of reading since 1957. Featuring award-winning authors and illustrators and a fabulous cast of beloved characters, I Can Read Books set the standard for beginning readers.

A lifetime of discovery begins with the magical words **"I Can Read!"**

Visit www.icanread.com for information
on enriching your child's reading experience.

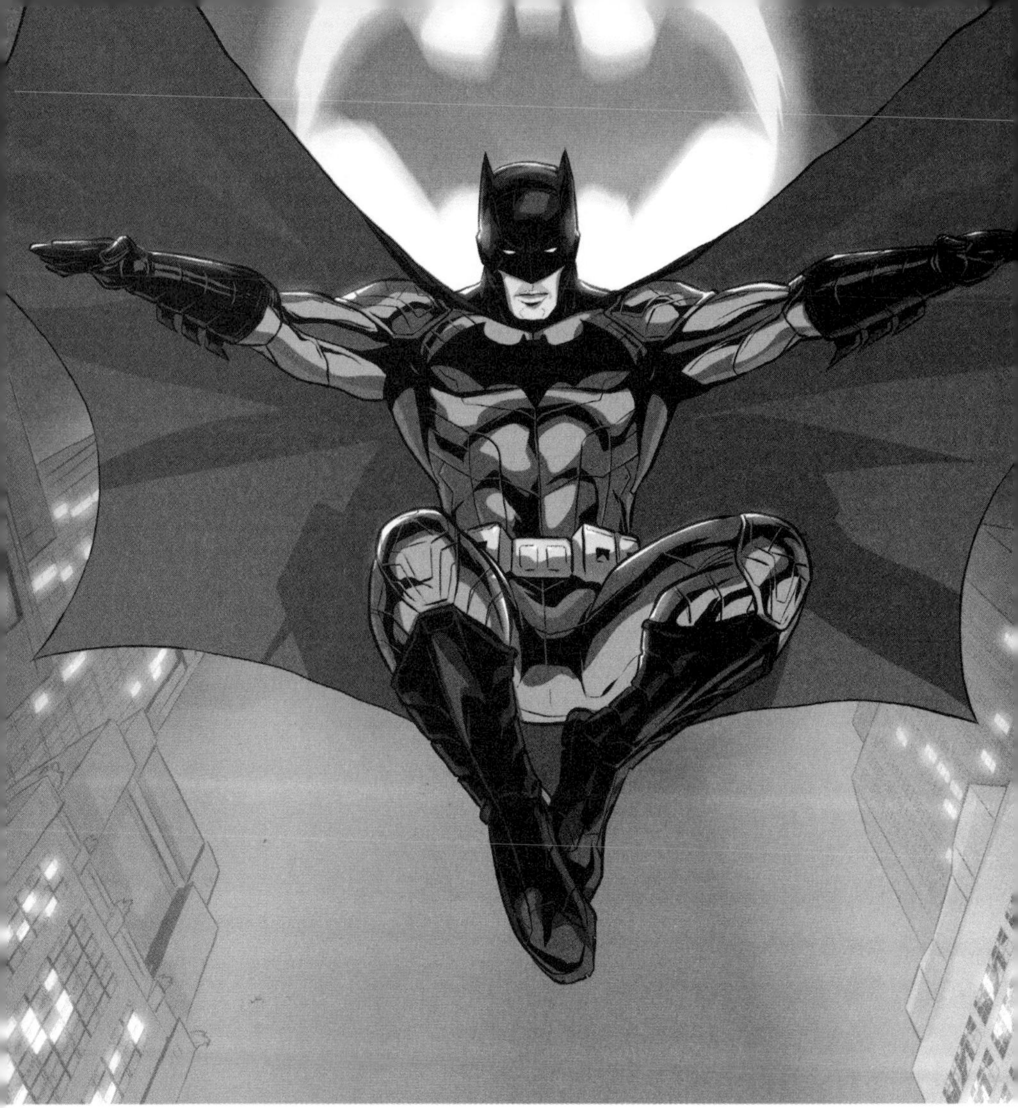

For information address HarperCollins Children's Books, a division of HarperCollins Publishers, 195 Broadway, New York, NY 10007.
www.harpercollinschildrens.com

Library of Congress Control Number: 2015961041
ISBN 978-0-06-236087-8

Book design by Victor Joseph Ochoa
16 17 18 19 20 LSCC 10 9 8 7 6 5 4 3 2 ❖ First Edition

I Can Read!™ READING 2 WITH HELP

BATMAN™

I AM BATMAN

by Delphine Finnegan
pictures by Andie Tong

Batman created by Bob Kane with Bill Finger

HARPER
An Imprint of HarperCollins*Publishers*

My name is Bruce Wayne.

I live in Gotham City.

I own Wayne Enterprises.

We build the best high-tech gadgets.

We make everything from huge planes

to the smallest computers.

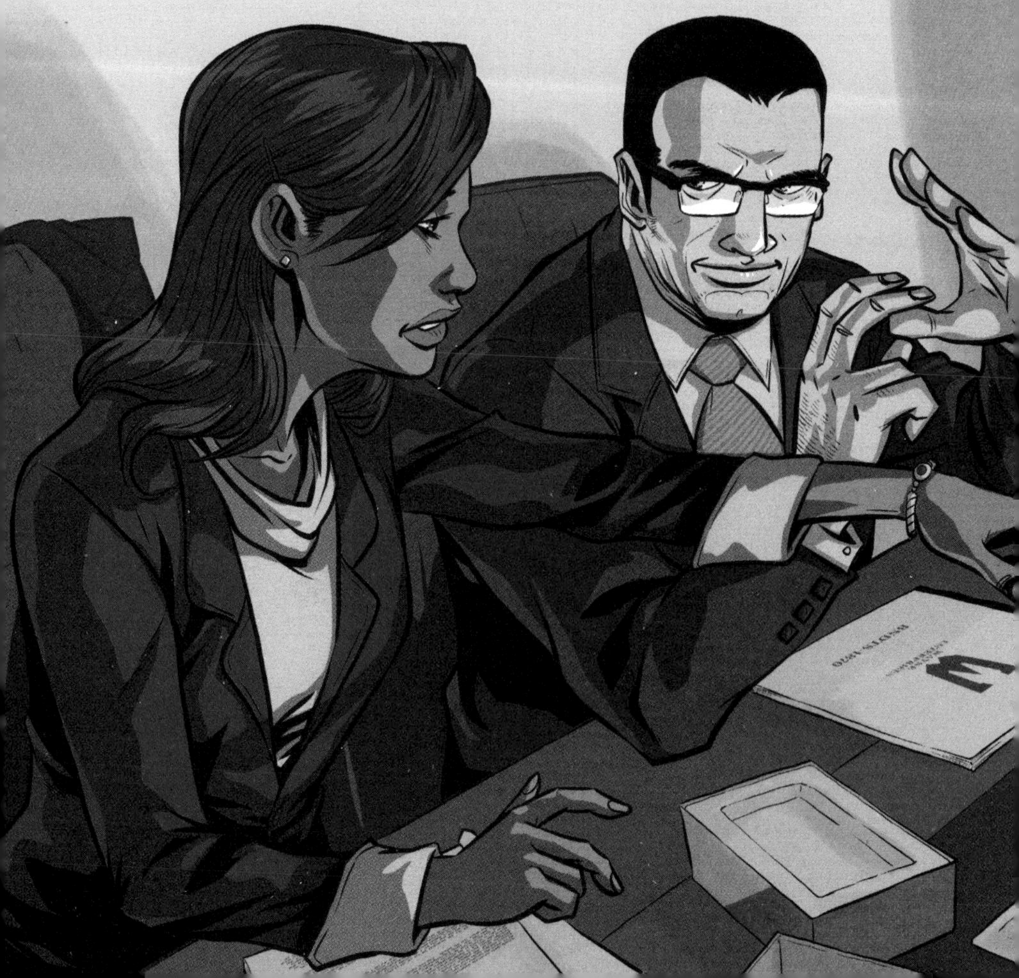

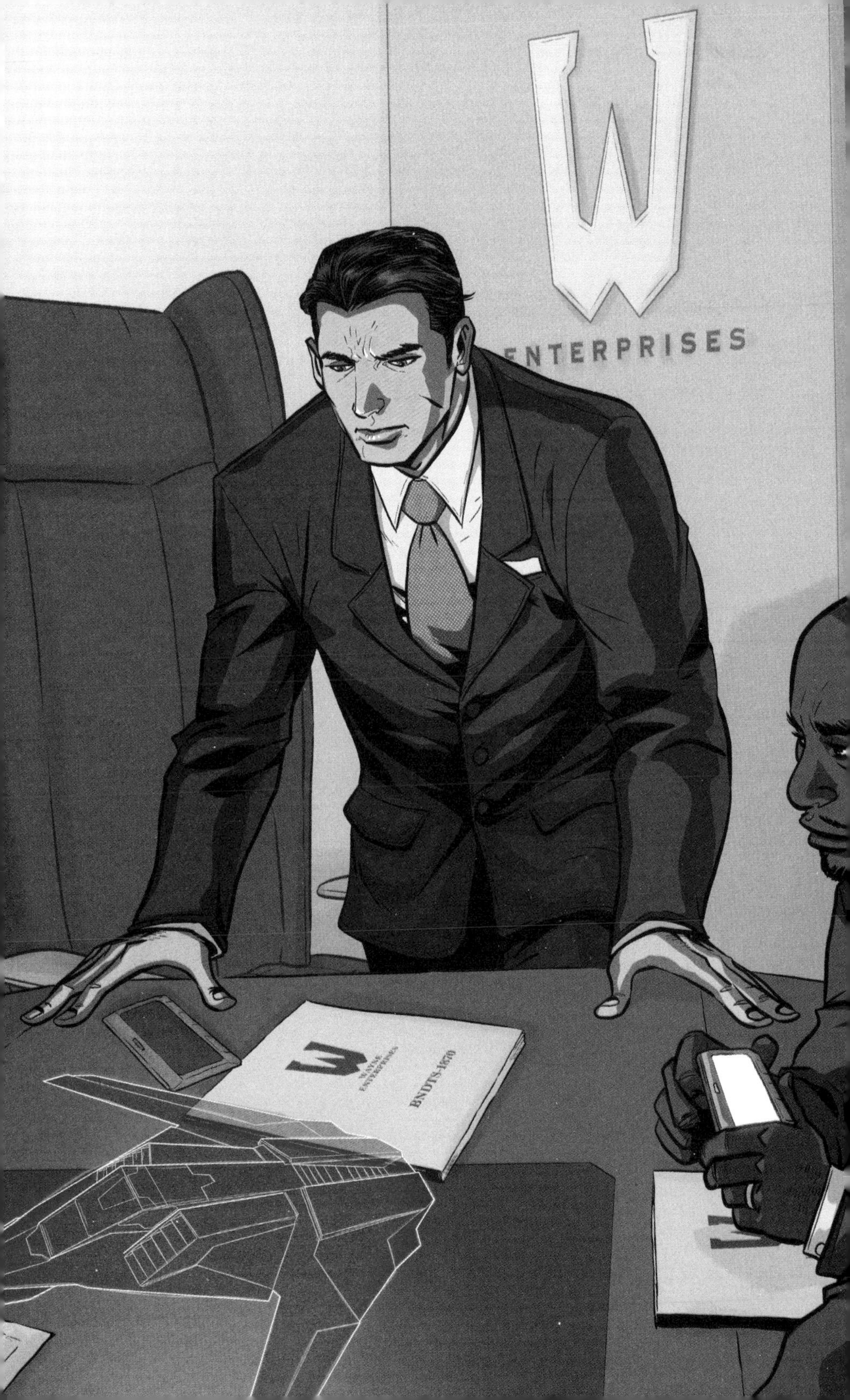
ENTERPRISES

This work is important to me.
I drive the best cars.
I use the newest gadgets.
I need these tools
day *and* night.

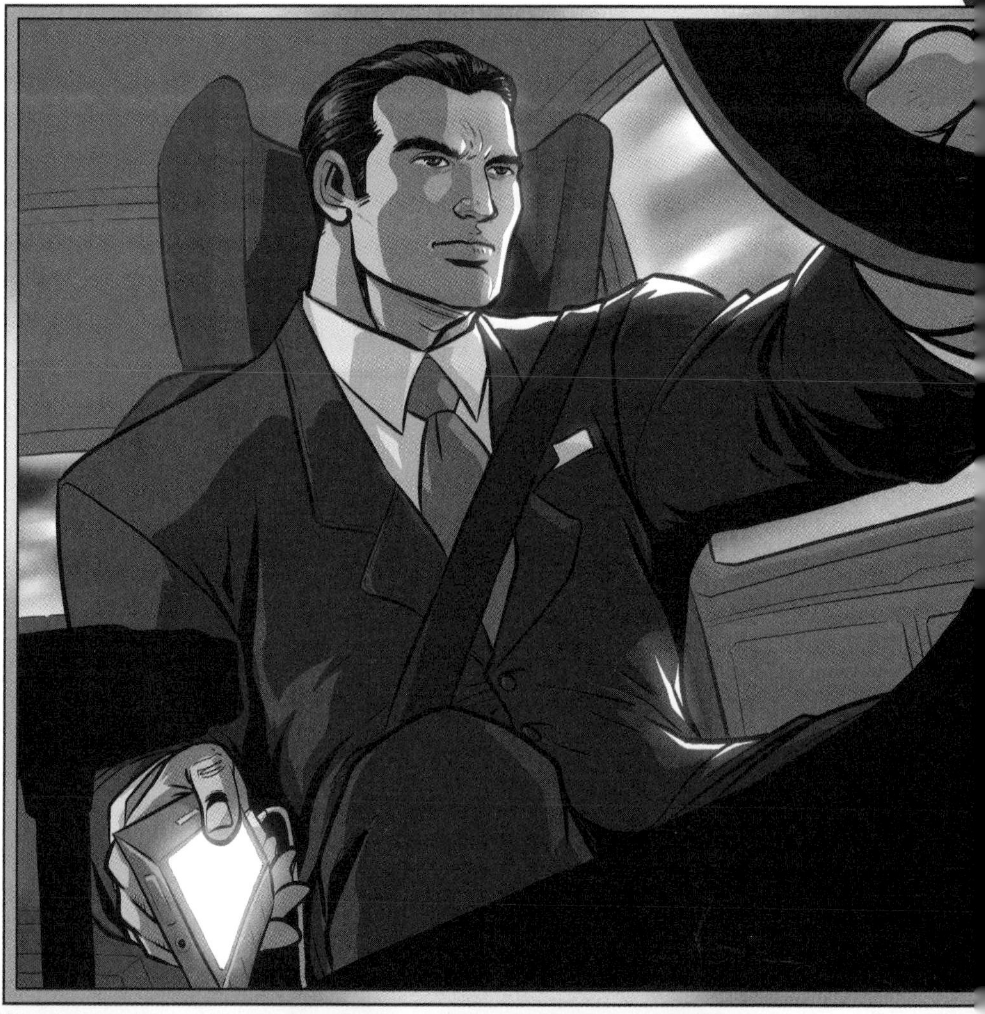

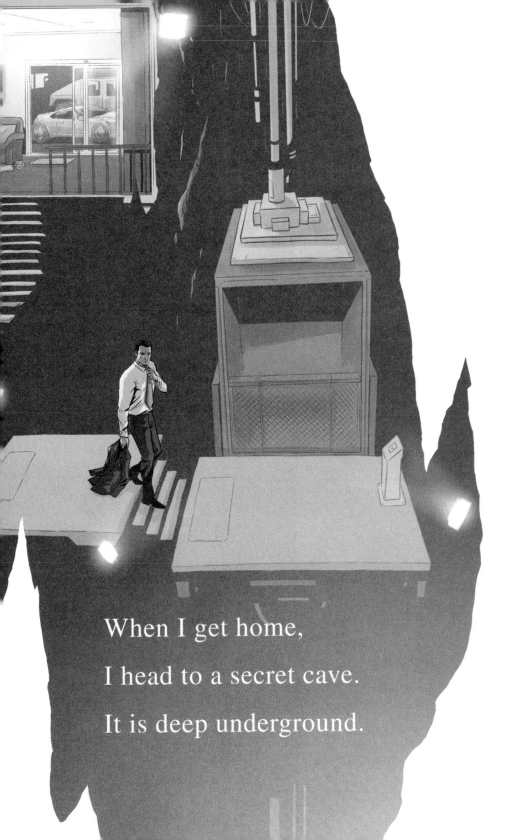

When I get home,

I head to a secret cave.

It is deep underground.

I am Batman.

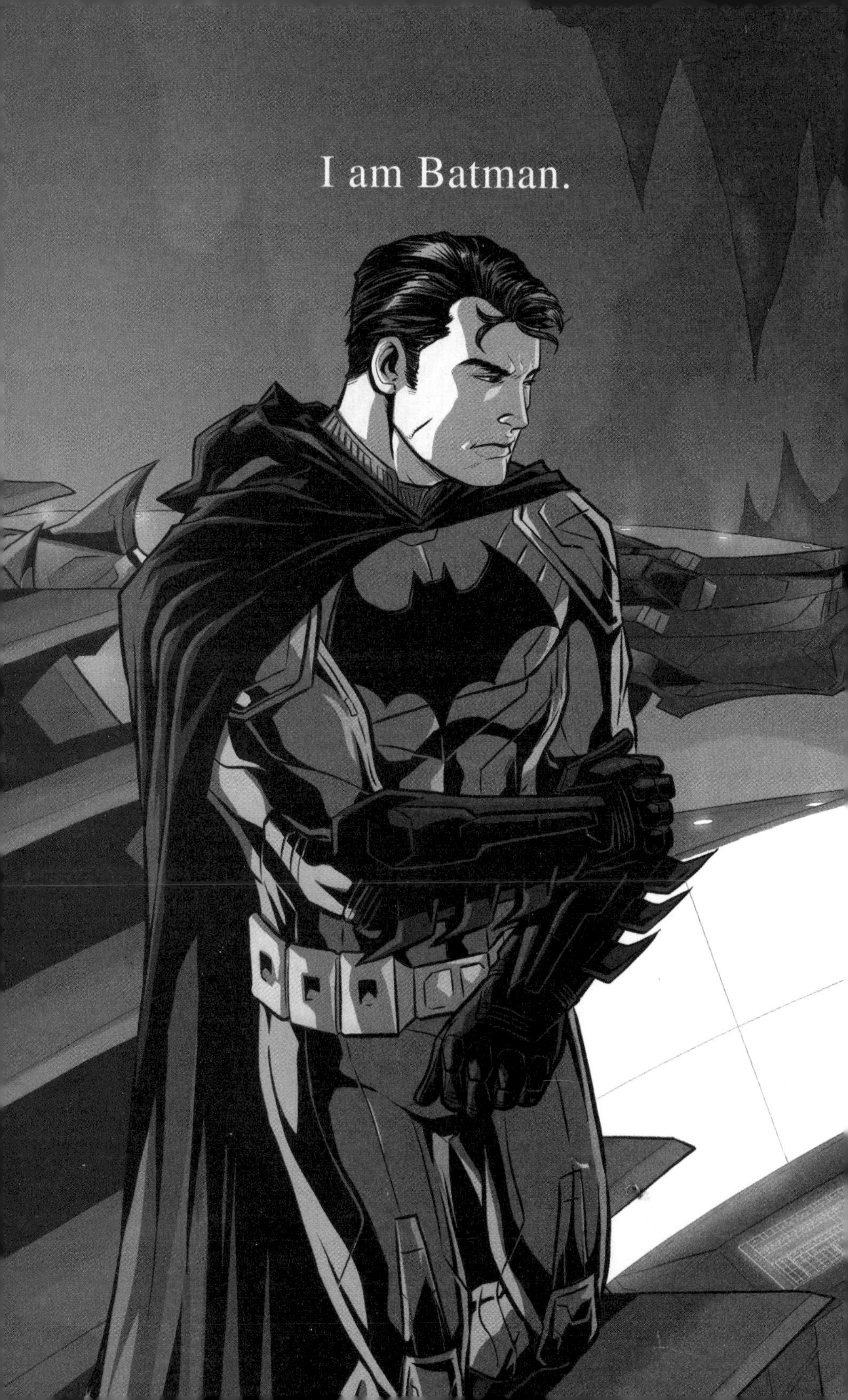

I keep watch over Gotham City.
My butler, Alfred, helps
keep my identity secret.

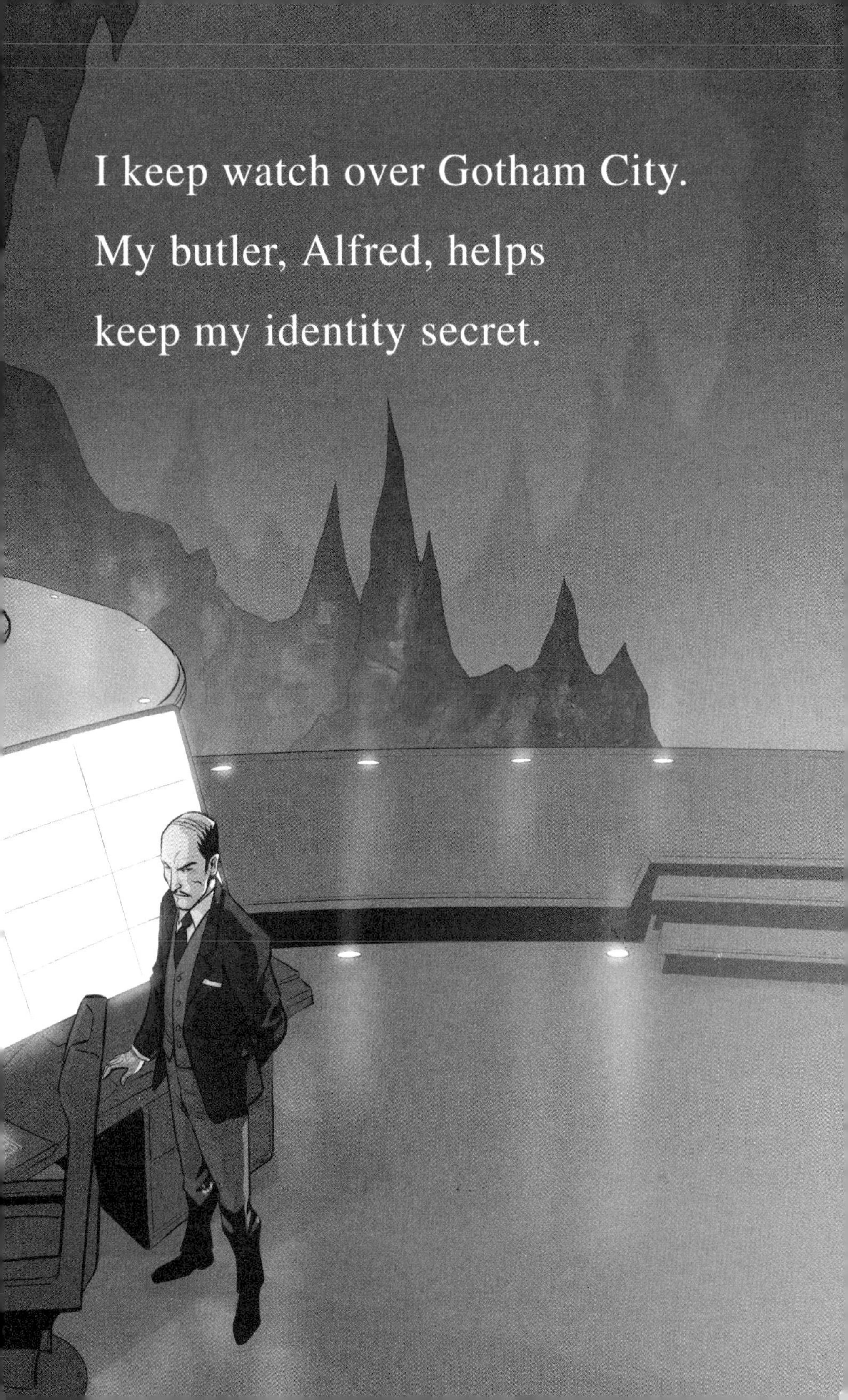

"Sir, you'll want to see this,"

says Alfred.

It is the Bat-Signal!

The Gotham City police send

this signal when they need my help.

My Batsuit and cape protect me.
My Utility Belt holds lots of gadgets.
I wear a mask
so no one knows who I am.

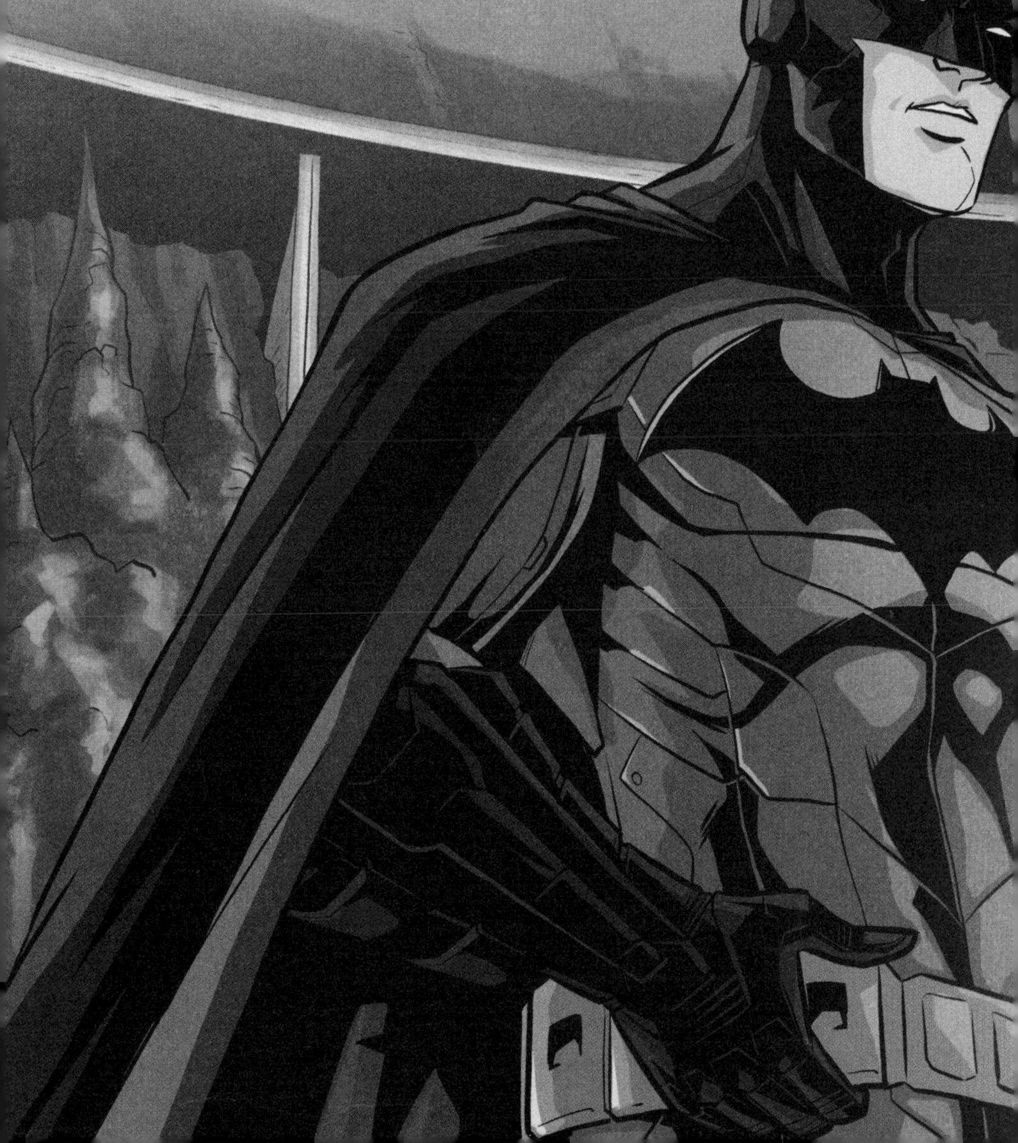

I jump into the Batmobile
and race into the night.

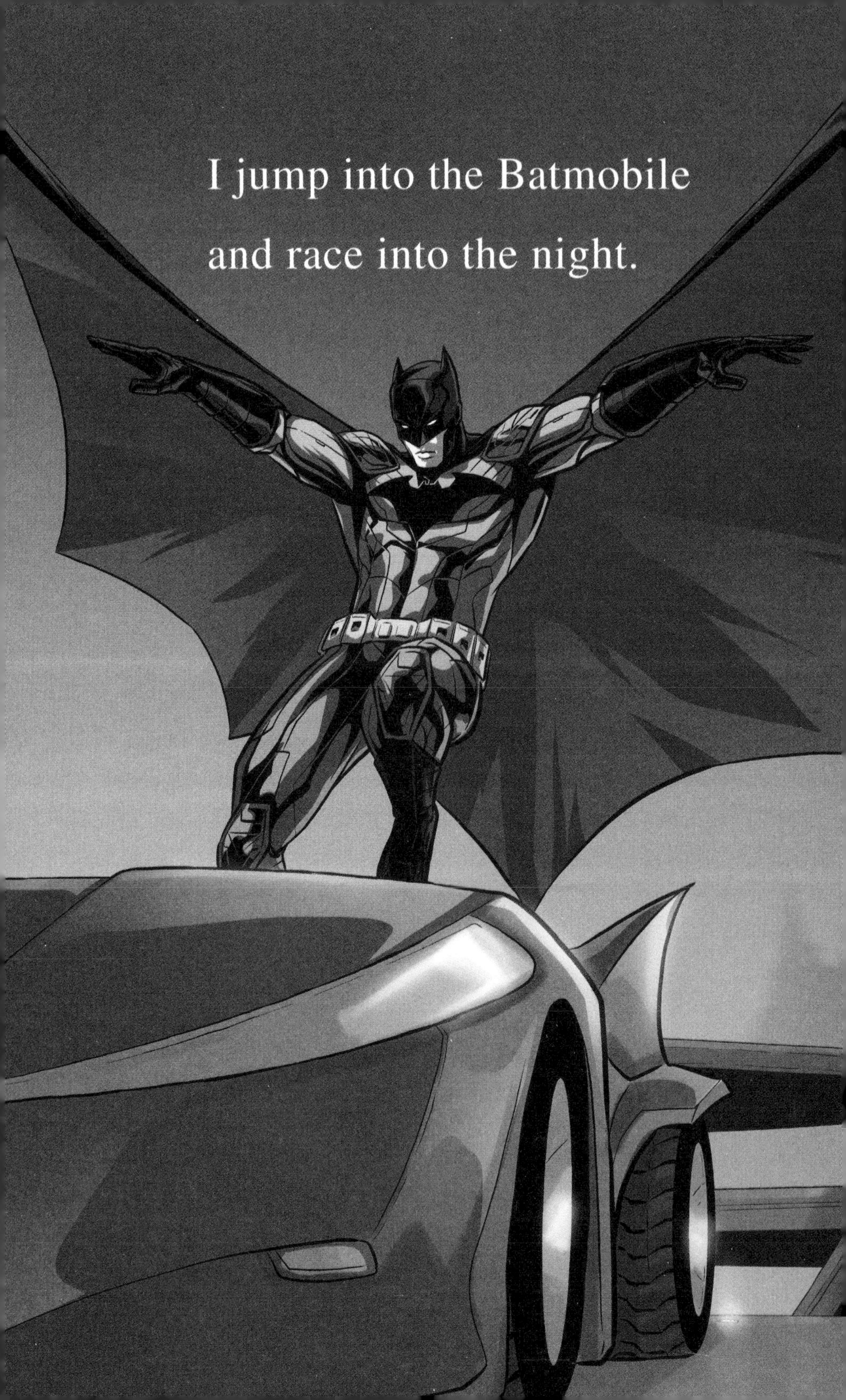

I contact Commissioner Gordon.
He is in charge
of Gotham City's police force.
"Something funny is happening
at the museum," he says.

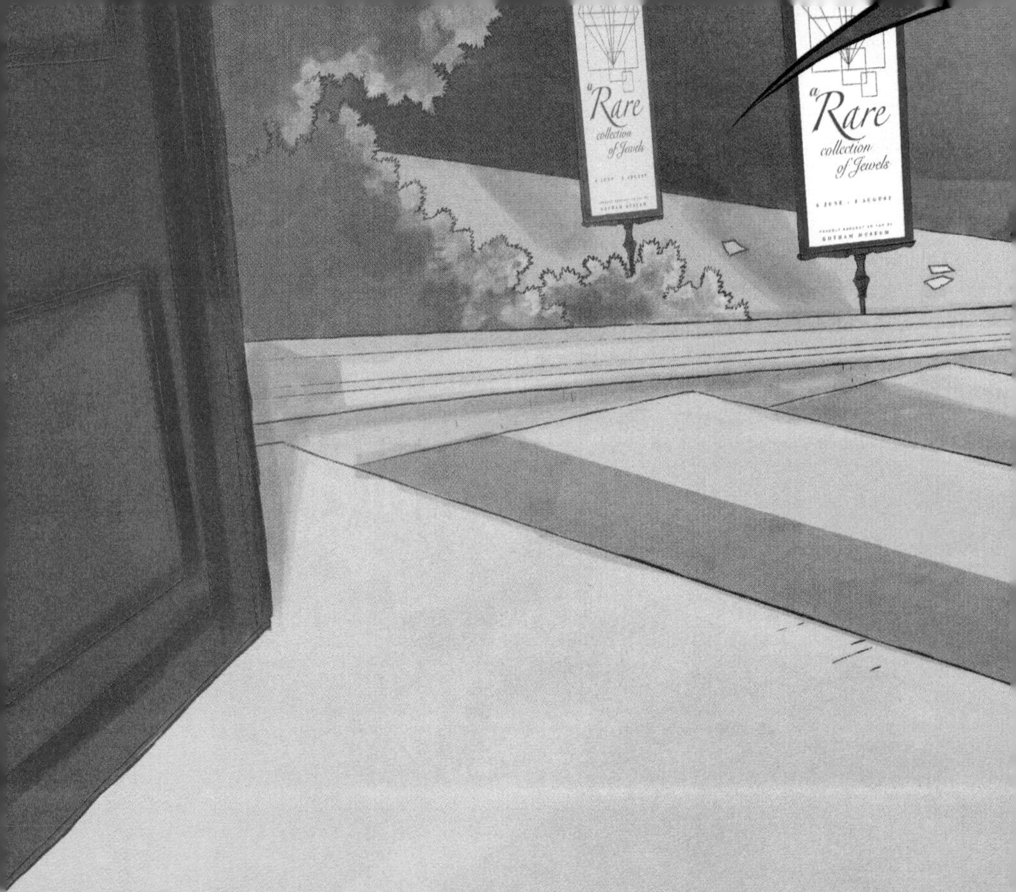
a Rare collection of Jewels
a Rare collection of Jewels

When I arrive,

I see a poster about a new exhibit.

The rarest jewels

will be on display.

The show opens tomorrow.

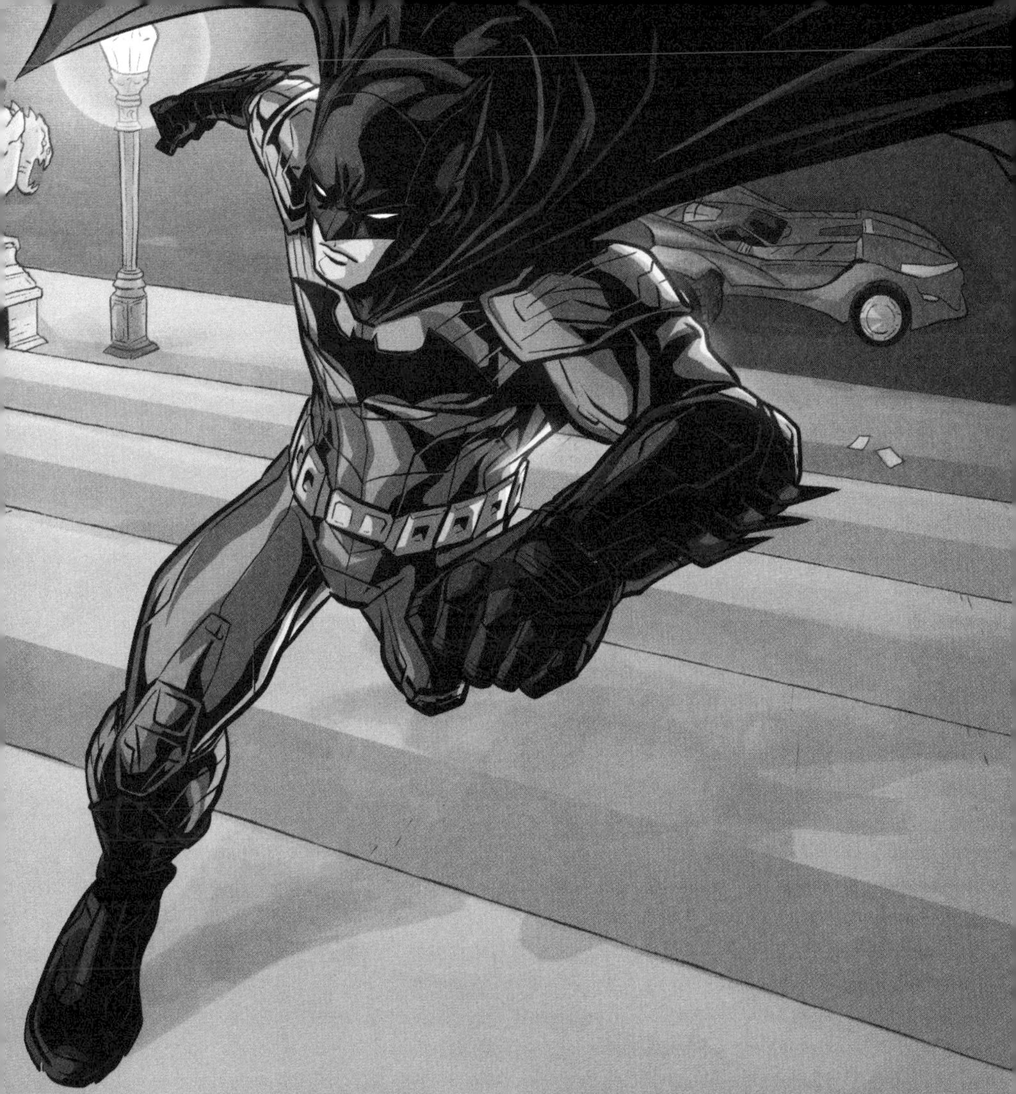

I also see something strange.

The museum doors are wide open.

The alarm is broken.

All of the guards are gone.

I head to the main hall
and find the guards.

"This should do the trick," I say.

Suddenly, a net falls down.

"Trick's on you, Batman!"

It's the Riddler!

He's not alone.

Catwoman and the Joker

make it a trio of trouble.

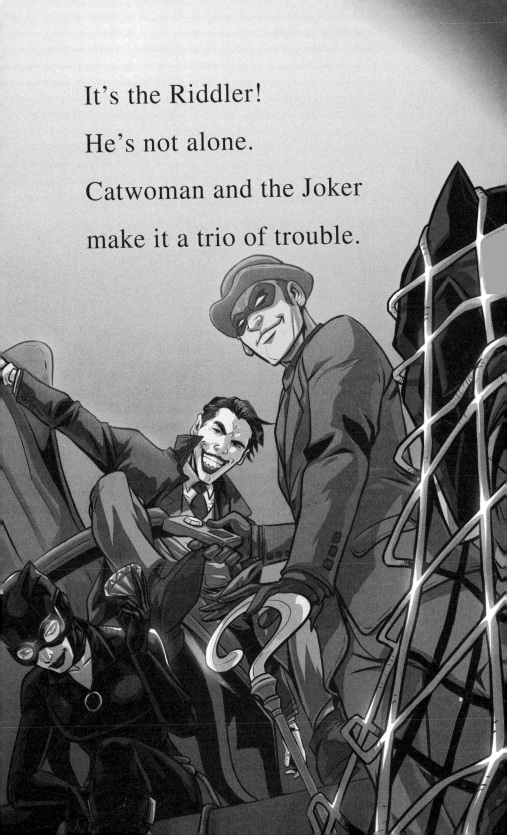

I twist and turn.

I try to get unstuck

from the net

while the three thieves

pack their bags.

I get free and grab my Batarangs.

Zip!

One slices the rope.

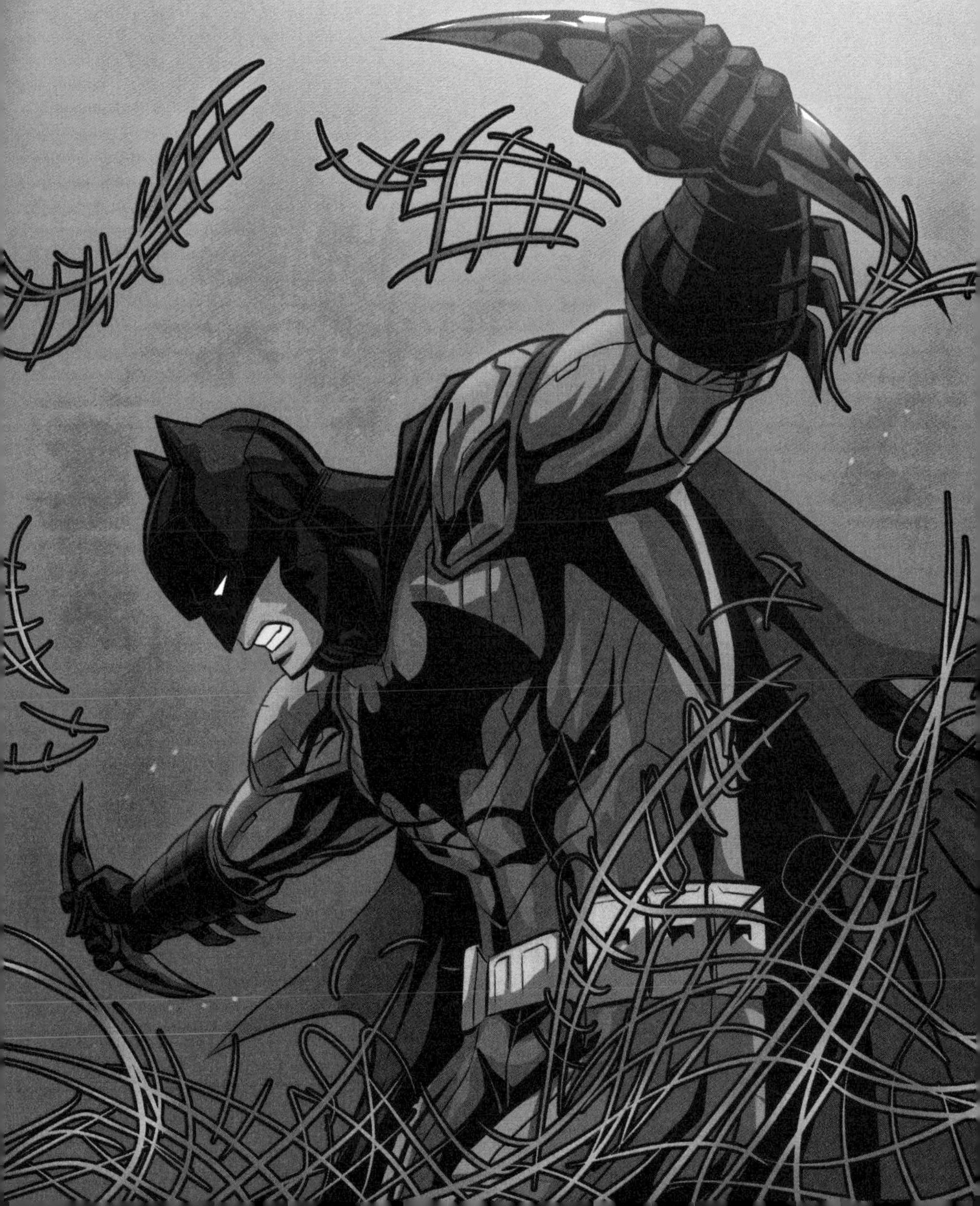

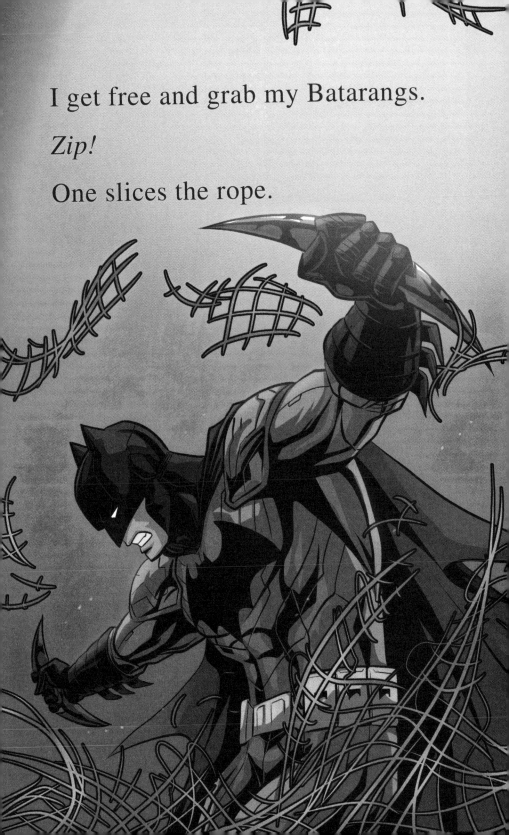

Zap!

I throw the other at the Riddler.

It stops him in his tracks.

But the Joker and Catwoman

get away.

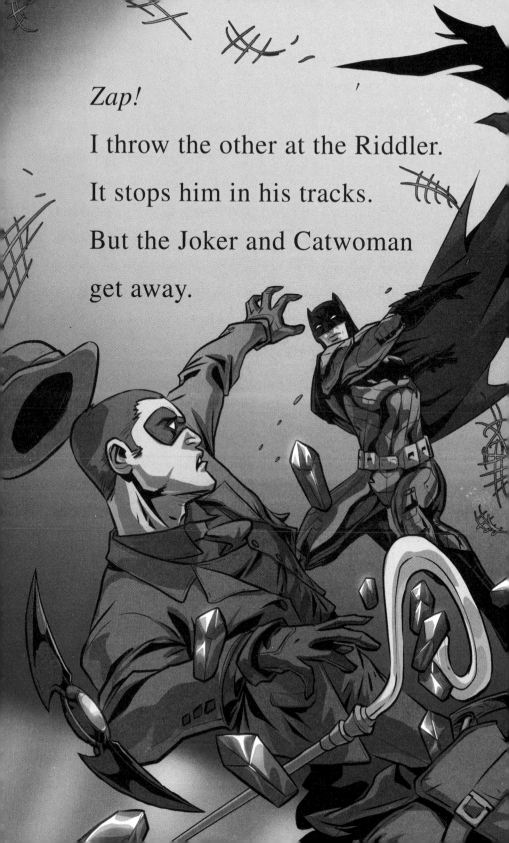

"Call Commissioner Gordon.
Tell him I'll get this duo soon,"
I shout to the guards.
Then I follow the two fiends.

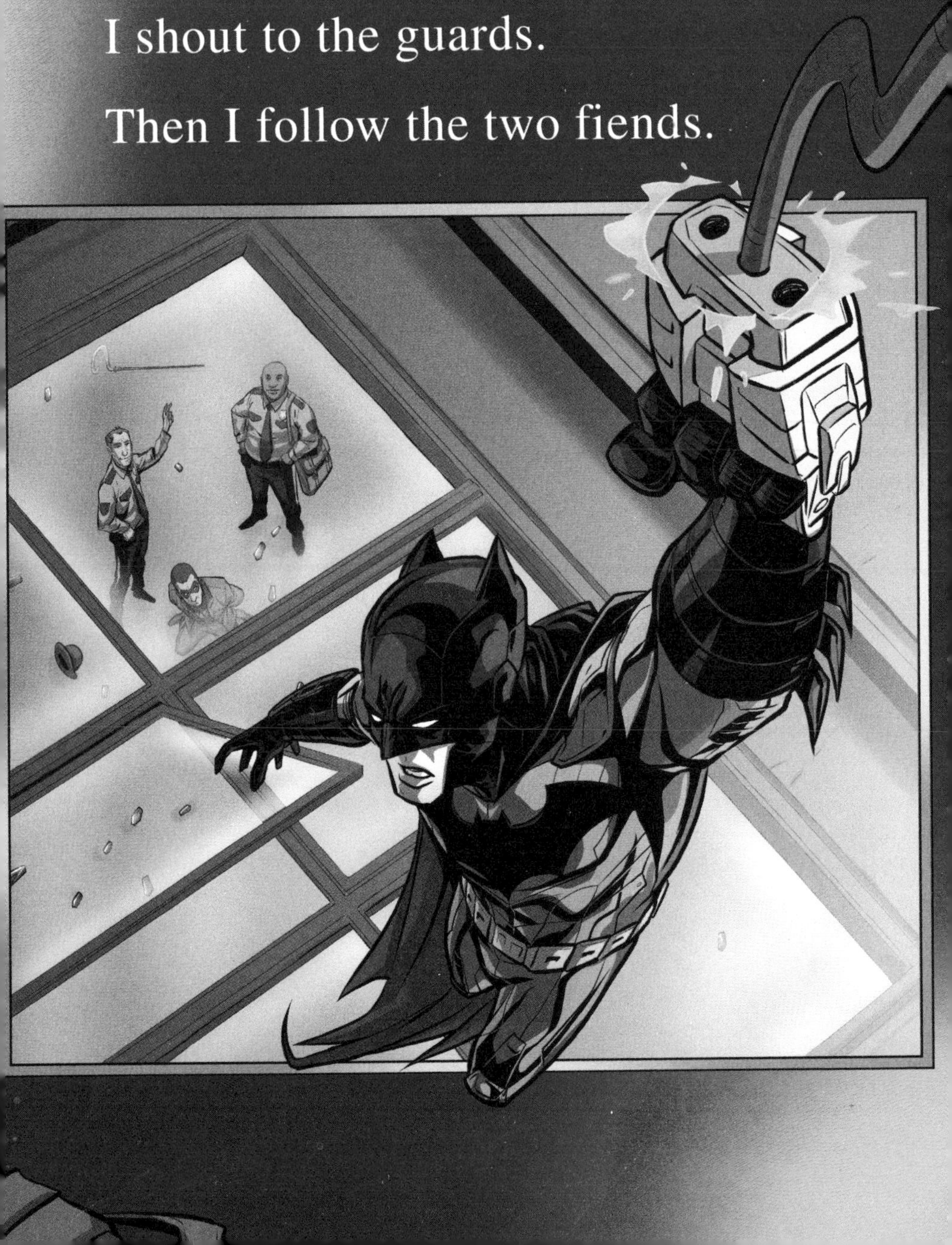

The Joker hitches a ride
from his crew.
Catwoman runs the other way.
"You have to pick a path,"
calls Catwoman.

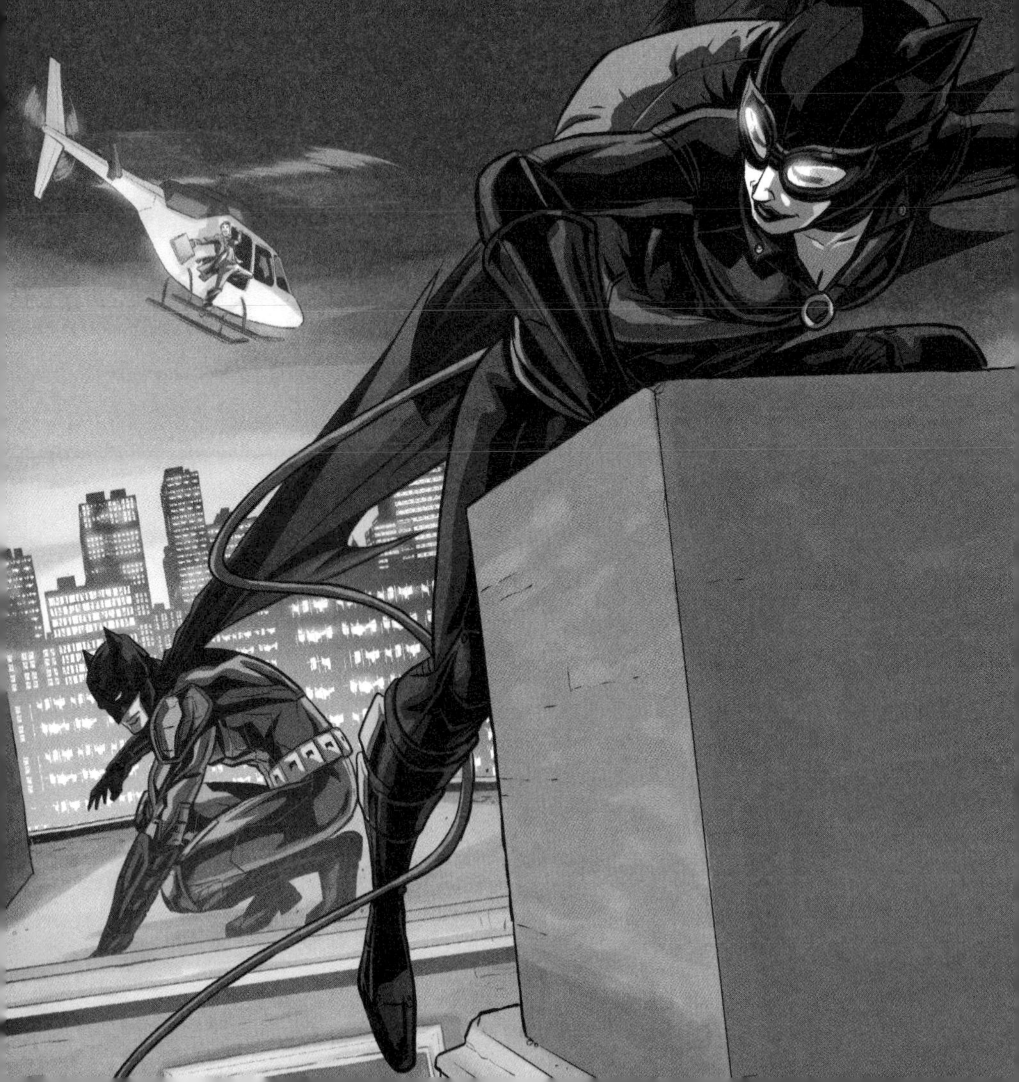

I toss a tracer

at the Joker's helicopter.

It's a direct hit.

Then I follow Catwoman.
I chase her until
there is nowhere left to go.

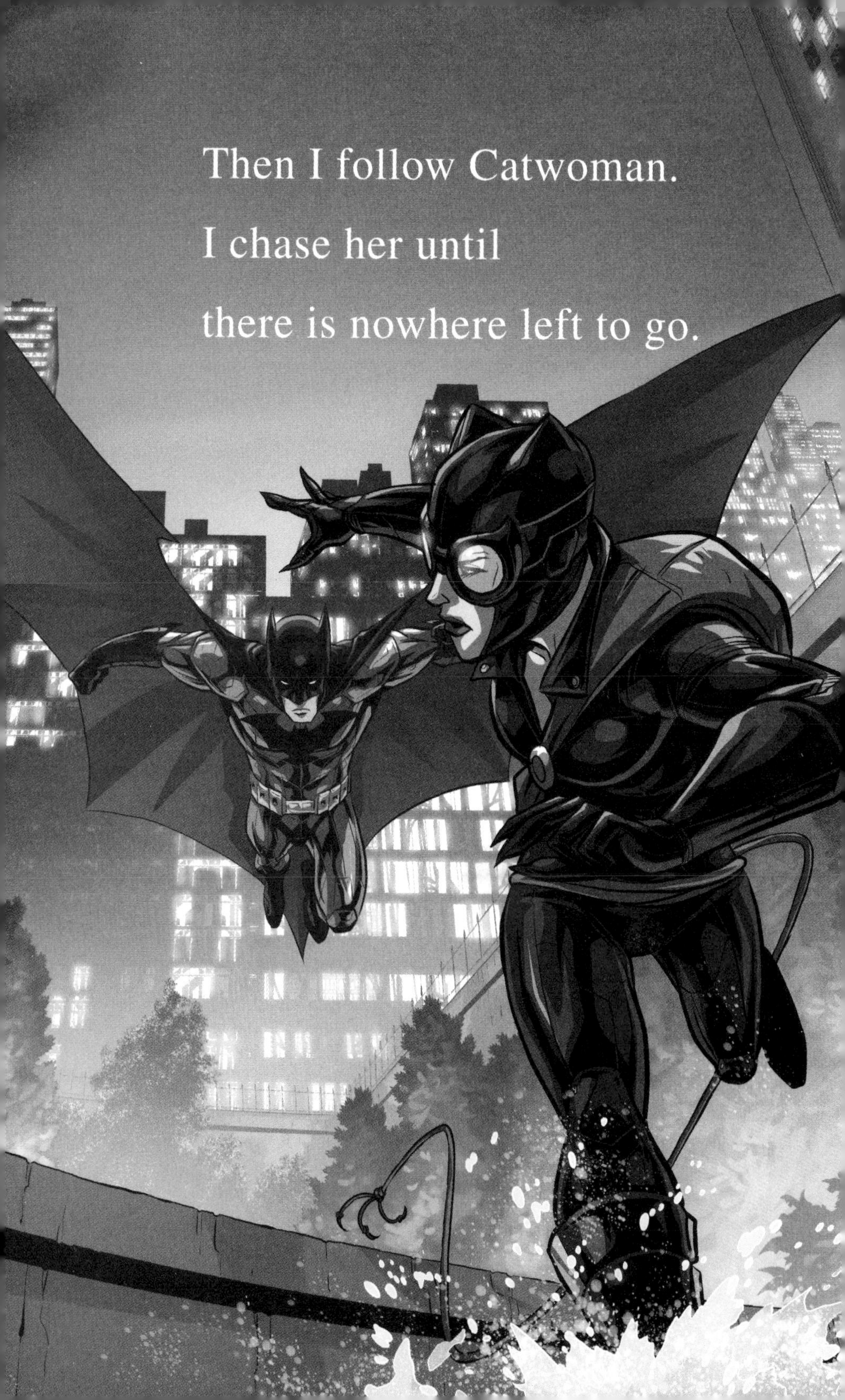

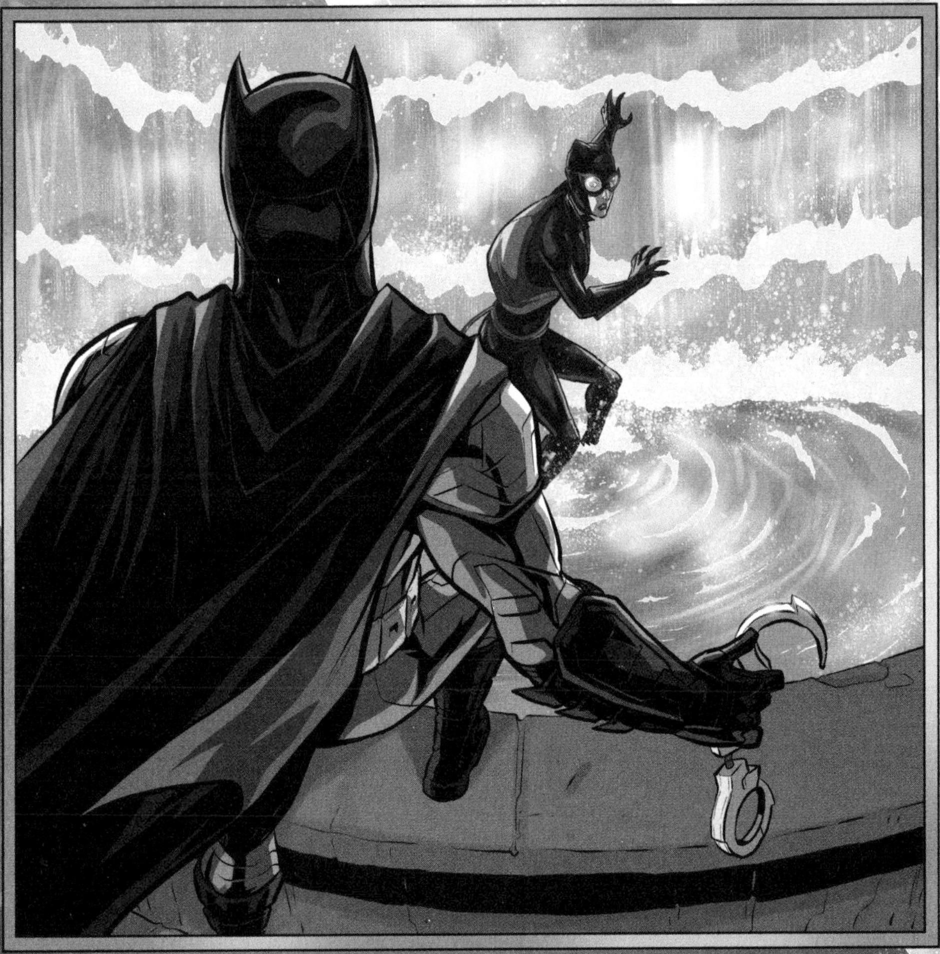

Cats don’t like water.

“You’re cornered, Catwoman!”

I say.

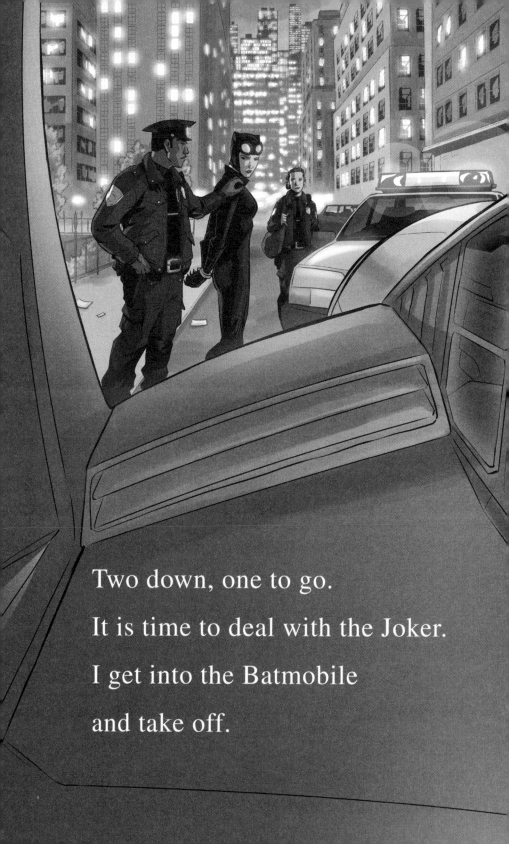

Two down, one to go.

It is time to deal with the Joker.

I get into the Batmobile
and take off.

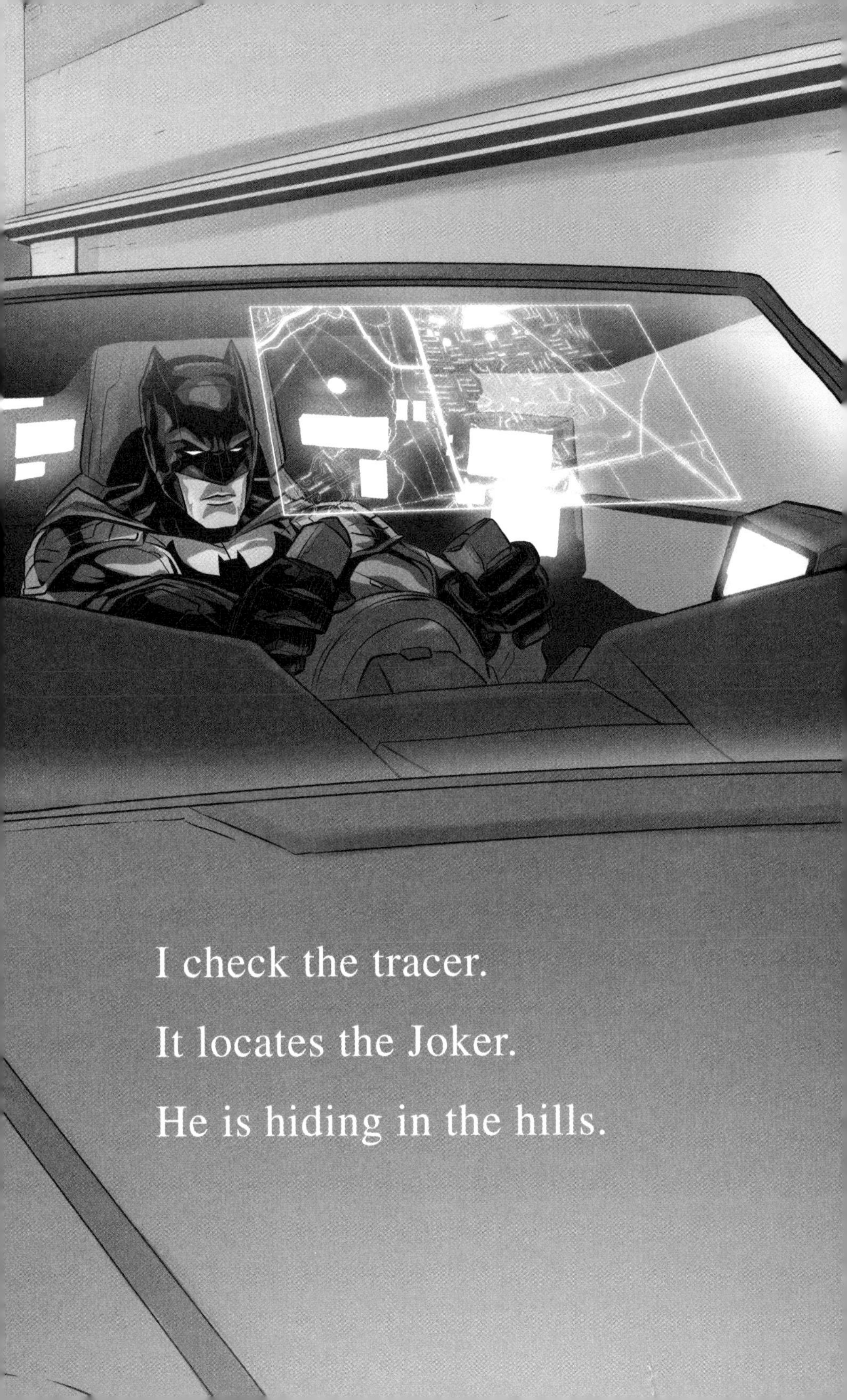

I check the tracer.

It locates the Joker.

He is hiding in the hills.

The Joker throws a party

at his hilltop hideaway.

He shows his loot to his crew.

He tells joke after joke.

I wait for the right time to strike.

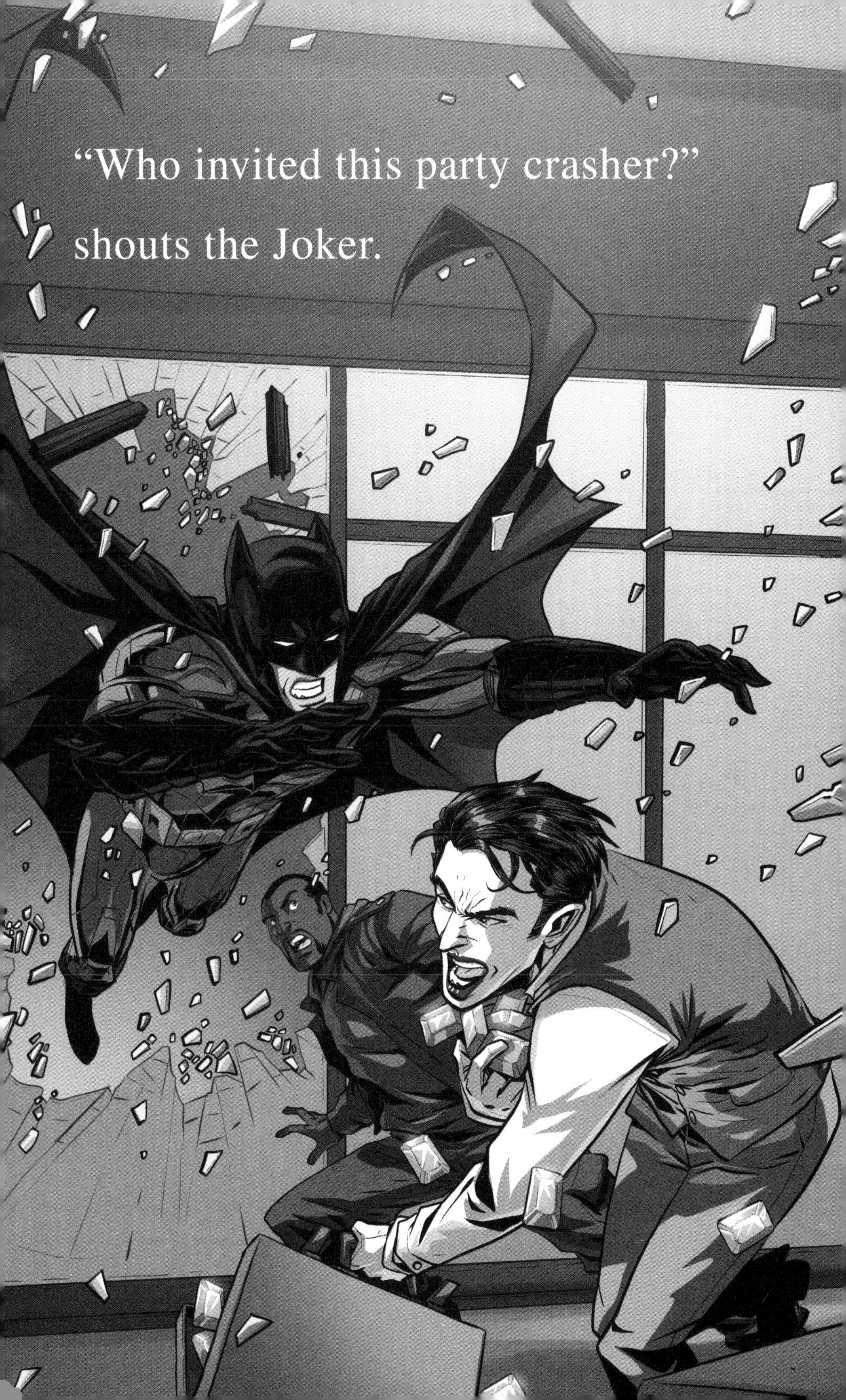

“Who invited this party crasher?” shouts the Joker.

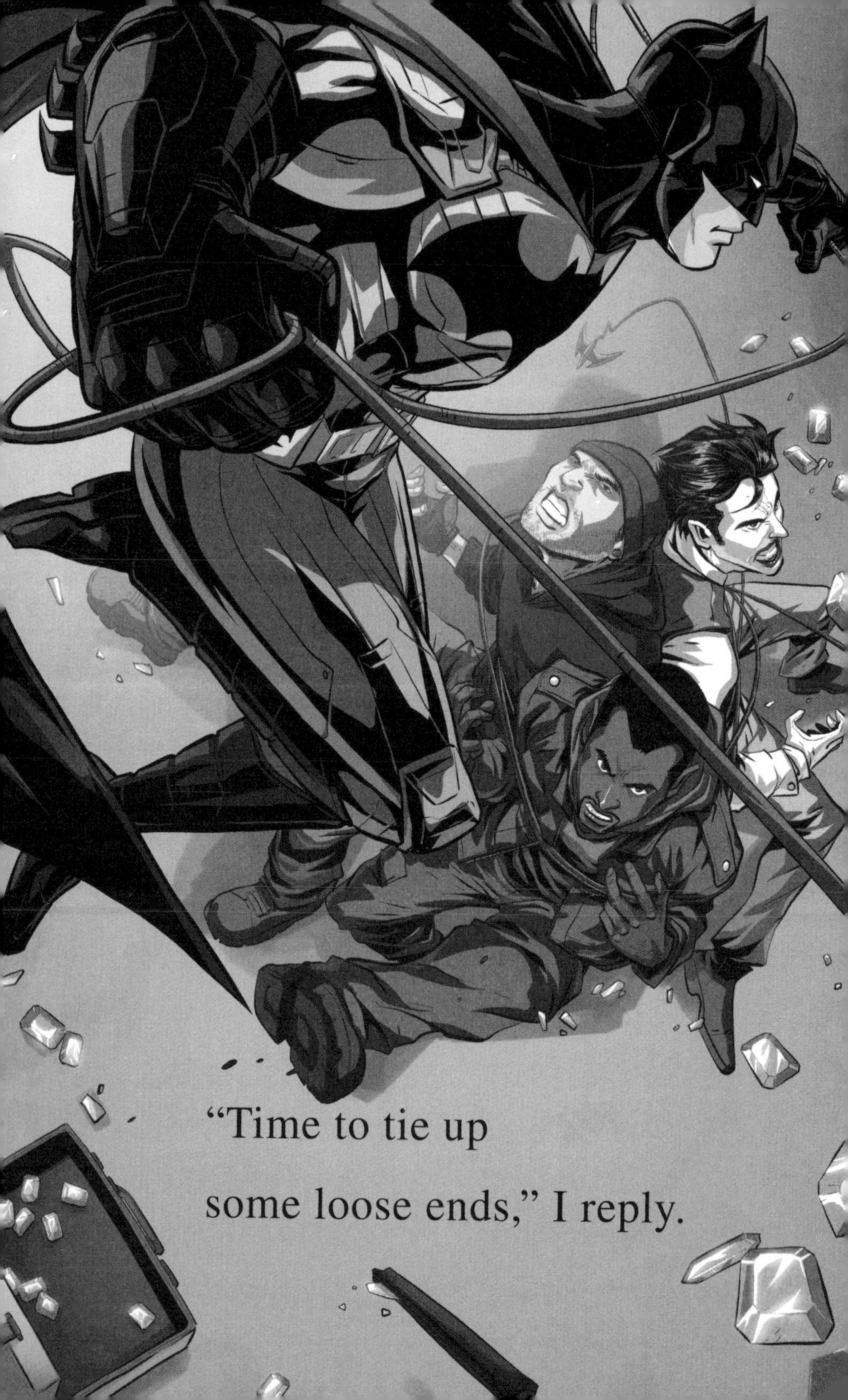

"Time to tie up
some loose ends," I reply.

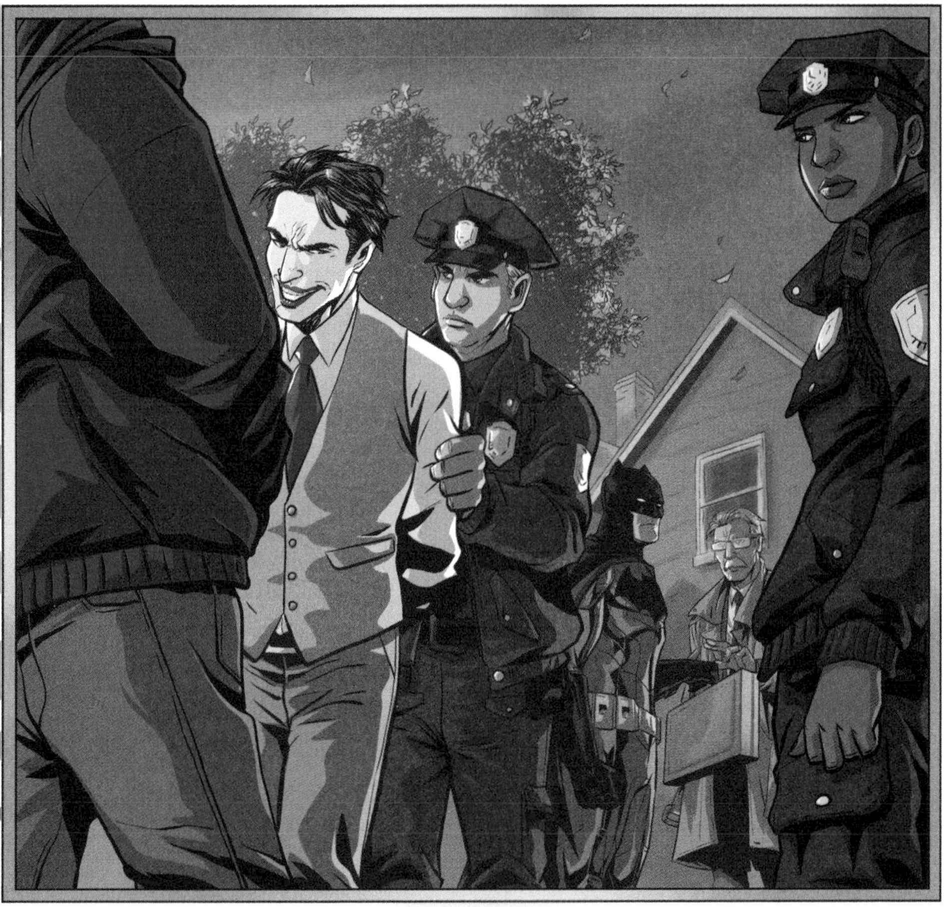

The Gotham City police arrive.
The trio of trouble
will be safely behind bars
and the jewels will return
to the museum.

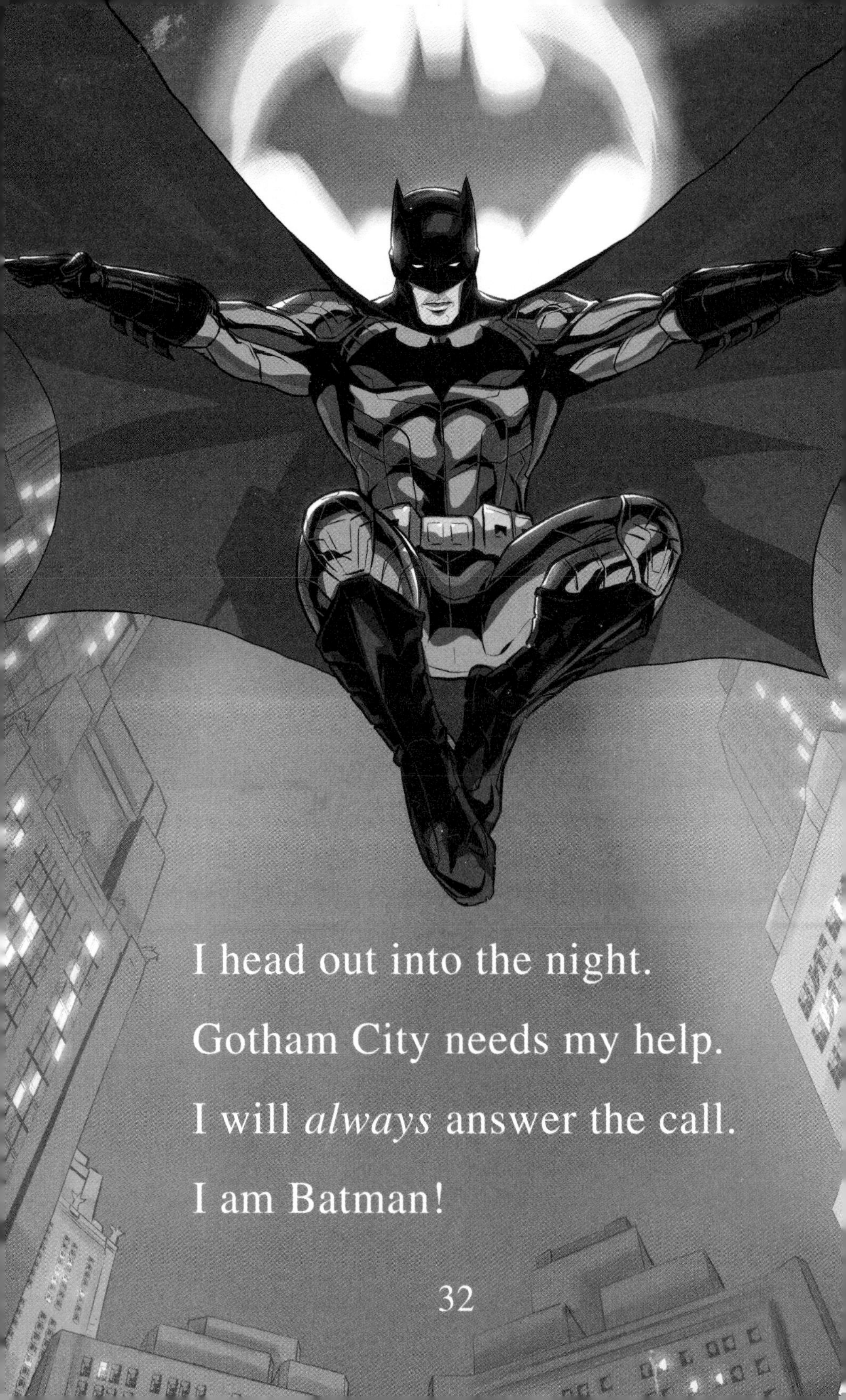

I head out into the night.

Gotham City needs my help.

I will *always* answer the call.

I am Batman!